A Strange Journey

Harold Wynne

ISBN: 978-1-3999-2645-4

DEDICATION

I would like to thank, from the bottom of my heart, the Carer's, Support Staff, Doctors, Nurses of Our Lady's Hospice and Care Services and St Luke's Hospice, without support from them, that darkness they call cancer may have overwhelmed us to a state where we were no use to anyone.

I would also like to thank my family, my Ma, Lorraine, Mark, Derek, Angela, Julie, Joanne, Rebecca, Danielle, Kathy, Karen, Craig, Luke, Jade, Becki, Shannon, Mary and all my extended family and friends, for showing courage in the face of overwhelming battles.

I would also like to thank my secret readers, Sandra and Sarah (I wasn't sure they could read).

Last but of no means least, my team in spirit (who got a raw deal, when they got me), the absolute beauty of the Angels, family in Spirit, Guides, Ascended Masters, Healers and all the beings of Light, The Virgin Mary and God.

Special mention to Lisa Elmas, my Teacher, my Friend, who took the time to teach me to connect with spirit.

CONTENTS

I. PREGNANT

The train was bleedin' late, so now Vicky was going to be late again. The rain wasn't late, though, and it drizzled all over the place, driven by the gentle breeze.

Tuesdays were boring; nothing to do on a Tuesday. There was never anything good on the telly, staring daydreamingly out of the window. Not into the outside world, but more like dreaming inside of yourself. That was when she noticed the butterfly. Oh no, you can't be serious, you're wrong?

She was late by about three weeks or twenty-three days, to be exact; she was never late!

(Except for trains).

The day went by in a haze of doubt and she thought a good night's sleep would fix her and maybe bring on her yokes.

The next morning, half a head brushed with one leg in the tracksuit, she was in a tizzy sitting on the bed. She had been told by doctors that she could not conceive or would at least need help to do it, so precaution was thrown to the wind like her knickers thrown onto the floor.

Where would she put a baby? She didn't even have a cot. What would her ma say? She would be a Granny. Definitely keeping the baby. She'd have to stay at work...maybe the butterfly was not meant for me or it meant something else? Or not even for me at all.

She didn't plan for this to happen, not until she was at least thirty or maybe even older. It just didn't make sense – preggers! Those mad, other women do that, no way. Her ma would have a canary.

Where would she start? Well, she knew it started as such, but when the bump arrived then everyone would know, She'd have to start eating healthy, maybe even go vegan?

Ah, but she did love the oul bit of meat, ha. Would she have to give up smoking and drinking? Probably, if she wanted the baby to be alright. What if there was something wrong with it; what if it looked like the Da? Ha-ha, she hoped not.

Sure, fuck it. I'm not giving up the fags and drink. Sure, the placenta was like a sponge and it would soak up any bad stuff. Wonder what I'll name it? She supposed that kinda depended on whether it was a boy or a girl...might call her after her cousin, Sarah.

It was Aunty June that was coming through. In fairness, she liked the name; she thought she liked it cos she had liked her cousin. Sarah was a lovely girl. She had died from one of them rare forms of cancer, that bastard of a disease that you wouldn't wish on your worst enemy. Sarah was a nice name, but Vicky might just use some of the name and call her Sorcha or Sandie or something like that.

"Eh," she said to the Spirit, "You are ata fuckin ruining it, I might as well just go out and buy all the clothes in pink now!"

It didn't really matter as June was gone now. She was prolly back in Mogan where she spent an awful lot of time in her apartment, she would be on the balcony in the blazing heat with her boobs hanging over the balcony. Vicky often said it to her about her topless antics on the balcony and she would say to me, "If you have it, flaunt it."

Talking to June was like talking to someone who was standing behind you and then they put a picture in front of your eyes and you got a feeling from it. Sometimes she would say some odd stuff to Vicky that she would not understand in that instant, but in time it was usually revealed to her; sometimes it took a long while, but it always came through. Sometimes it was a bit odd when they connected with Vicky. Like one time she was in eating a sandwich and a brew and she never knew when they are going to pop in to say hello, but they never frightened the shite outa her. The drizzle had now stopped, forgotten about like the knickers now under the bed.

II. UNCLE TOMMY

Tommy wanted to go for a pint or ten; it had been a very hard day spent hanging wallpaper, which wasn't his favourite thing in Inferior Decorating, as he called it. He fuckin hated them patterned rolls of wallpaper. Pain in the arse, they were, and usually you had to do the job for some pain in the arse. What was it with people putting patterned wall paper in the hall stairs and landing anyway?

"I'm not afraid of falling, it's the sudden stop that kills ya," he thought.

Mrs Murphy's house the last three days, it took forever and a day to strip that poxy wood chip wallpaper off the walls as it had seven layers of paint and the last one was gloss, a shite colour, must have been found at the back of the shed and they didn't want to waste it, a shite colour. She was like his bleedin' shadow, he went upstairs and she went upstairs, he went out the back and she was already there hanging out clothes. He couldn't get rid of her. He'd admit that she had not been following him, but she should have been out at the shops or something. He gave her a price job, but he might add on a few bob for annoyance and the fact that she had seen all his tricks of the trade. He went for a pony and trap and when he was wiping, he half expected her to hand me the bog roll, ha.

"Jaysus, these shoes need to be reheeled. Do people still do that or just throw them out", he thought to himself. Now the plan was to walk the long way to the pub, to avoid all the leeches and scroungers, if that went to plan and if he wasn't hounded to buy tickets for some poxy raffle, then he'd have enough money to buy a few cosy pints and maybe even a short or two.

A big gravy belch came back up to haunt his tonsils – mash, gravy mince and peas, no Michelin stars, but you could shovel it into ya, like a Cavan man at a free buffet. He had done just that with a big soup spoon. Forks were shite for this kind of stuff unless you wanted to wear some gravy on your shirt.

The price of a pint had gone up last week; why the fuck don't they just leave drinking men alone? "I pay my taxes, don't I?" he wondered. "Well, most of the time I do. Well actually, that's a lie. I don't at all, but there's drinking lads down the bar paying a fortune in taxes, a voracious amount altogether and now an increase on the pint, I'll be dead before I see it going down." A quick glance up at the sky before he pulled open the bar door seemed to suggest that the walk home would be nice and dry, just like his throat was now. Dry as an Arab's sandal.

"A pint. Thanks, Paul. Where's the Eddy lad tonight, on his break again?" asks Tommy, "Nope, he's out back having a smoke and probably reading the paper," said Paul as he left the pint to settle.

Tommy loved it here. A home away from home. A good oul Dublin boozer, none of those flashing lights and all that shite that goes on in town.

He took a good sip of his pint and headed over to the lads in the big booth. The ole lads called it the Departures Lounge, as all of its occupants were on the way out or had one foot in the grave, so to speak.

Eddy was a head case for a barman, absolutely great crack and a diamond rated slagger. He was always slagging the boys in The Departure Lounge. He would say stuff like, "Eh, lads. Just to tell you, the Doc said no slate or tic for them lads in the big booth." Then he would laugh his head off saying, "Sure we are going to go someday, aren't we lads?"

The barmen had swapped places and it was Paul's

turn to have some tea and read the paper.

Tommy called for another and Eddy was on it like a light and brought it down to him. No one else got that kind of service, except the oul lads. Tommy had taken a mouthful from the second pint and now the crack and the stories had started; the lads were recalling funny stories. Now, as the lads knew, there were rules for telling stories in the pub. When the lad had one to four pints on board, you could talk about stuff like the football, and the weather (but only if it was extreme, like if you ended up with two trampolines in your garden with the kids still bouncing on them from the wind), there were also murders (but not from America, as they do lots of killing every single day and never take a day off from killing), especially local murders, scummers getting caught red-handed with loads of contraband and their ill-gotten gains, and, as always, there was the increase on the price of the sacred pint.

Then there is the five-to-nine-pint scenario, which was Tommy's favourite time to tell a yarn or two.

Ding-dong piped up to start off storytime. (His name was Denny, no one knew where his nickname came from and no one prolly cared either, he prolly got it from selling stuff door to door, ringing doorbells.) Now, here lies another strange thing that really happened a lot in Dublin. I am not saying that it didn't happen in the country, but it was not as common and I had never seen this trait abroad, either. Before Ding-dong gets going, he barely has a word or two out, Sharkey cuts in front of him (another thing that wasn't done in good company).

"Did ya hear about the young lad who got whacked walking down the road not too far from here? He was shot by a pillion passenger off the back of a motorbike. Young lad did not die straight away. If it were me, I would have sung like a canary before I died and sent the fuckers to jail," said Sharkey. The lads were well used to Sharkey, his bark was worse than his bite. The lads tell a great story, when he was not there of course, of how he started a row in a snooker hall and when all hell broke loose, he slipped out the side door. He was supposed to have three chickens as his coat of arms.

"Do you remember, Tommy? When the wife brought down my dinner, knife and fork and all as I was busy having a few pints and I couldn't make it home?"

"Do I remember? Sure, I can still remember the taste of it, and Eddy bringing over the salt and pepper and asking if she's going to bring down the desert," he said, laughing.

"Ah, the good oul days. I wouldn't mind a bit of that dinner now, instead of these poxy peanuts, all they do is get stuck in your teeth," Sharkey said.

By now The Departures Lounge boys were in full swing and on a roll telling story after story, lie after lie (the strange thing is that lies were actually allowed to be told if they made people laugh).

Tommy called for a small one – this was a sign that he was a good few in or around eight pints at this stage – with a drop of water as he wasn't paying extortionate prices for a drop of lemonade. He wanted to drink here, not buy the place.

As the boys all knew, you had to keep abreast of the man beside you. As when drinking among company, it was considered rude to overtake another drinker. Unless, of course, you had a reason. Dave looked at Tommy.

"what?" said Tommy, "I've had a fuckin hard week of graft." That was it, an excuse was given, drink away. The gargle had done its job and the lads were all mellowed out, with work, wives, and woe's the furthest thing from their minds.

Tommy leaned forward into the group, silence fell in the booth and excitement contained. Tommy was going to tell his story, the one he is famous for.

"Kentucky, many moons ago," he started, "at that time I was working state-side as there was no work over here. Nothing to do and the queue for the scratcher was a mile long – butter vouchers and tins of canned meat were being handed out too. The wife's first cousin, Liam, done a bit of painting and decorating over there, so it was staying here and doing nothing or going over and working for him. I was just a young lad at that time and about three stone lighter than I am today and had a shock of wavey healthy hair. I was in the early days of my drinking before I had settled on the pint and the short. We had just completed a huge job over there, on time and on budget. A stack of apartments we'd done and there was another stack waiting to be done, but I had to let off some steam first. All I was looking for was a little bar out of the way to have a skin full of drink before getting sucked into another huge job. All work and no play and all that jazz. I had a whole lot of cash burning a hole in my pocket.

"I got a ride to the local place where all the bars are – in the States they are mad, all the pubs are together in or around the same area. I hear some music from a long way off and found myself on Bar's Street. Exactly what I was looking for – some live music. I thought I had found a band, but it was a load of different lads taking to the stage one after another, some of them were okay and some of them played really great stuff like The Boss and Dire Straits and Neil Diamond and the like. The beer was really cheap. It wasn't as strong as ours, but it was cold and cheap. Did I already say cheap? I didn't stay on the beer for long before I moved onto the spirits. Bourbon, in fact. Ye know what they say, when in Rome. So, the music played on and I went to watch a game of pool between two local lads.

"These were my type of people, kinda like my friends in low places. So bourbon and branch water it was – branch water was just the stream that they got the water to make the bourbon from.

"The pool game was over and it didn't look like there were any more players, so I stepped forward and put my coins into the slot and racked up them balls. While I was setting up, a big black fella came over and said, 'Want to shoot some balls?' I said sure and he told me his name was Kelvin. He wasn't a pool shark. He was basically like me, a bad pool player but a good storyteller. So the balls rolled and the drinks flowed and he told he was ex-military, used to fly them choppers with supplies on them for the Marines. He had no horror stories to tell, so I presumed he must have been good pilot."

"Who is the bourbon for?" Although Paul knew who it was for, he just had to ask. If he left it there without saying someone would be getting a free drink. Tommy nodded, so Paul put it in front of him. He picked his story back up.

"Kelvin asked me what I was drinkin' and I told him. He took on sniff of my drink and said, 'That's donkey piss. Go up and order what I am drinking, tell him I sent you.' So doing as I was told I finished my donkey piss and headed to the bar to order two Kelvin specials, I knew by now that they didn't sell doubles in the States and walked away pouring two into one. The next few games of pool went by in a boozy blur. He won and then I won, then no one cared. One thing was for sure, the music was getting better as the night wound on.

"The bar ran out of the good bourbon that we were drinking so Kelvin said, 'I have an unopened bottle of Kentucky's finest back at my place not too far from here.' I told to him to lead the way and grabbed my coat and off we went into the dark Kentucky night. We walked for around fifteen minutes and then I followed him into his place. 'Shut the door,' he said, moving down the hallway. I came in but I didn't move from the hall door, he stuck his head around the corner and said to me, 'Come on in, we don't bite' while he was laughing.

"I walked down the hallway to the sitting room and in his hand he had a full bottle of the bourbon we were drinking in the bar. No mixers were needed now as it went straight down the hatch. I was sitting on a little two-seater sofa, so I just hung my jacket off the back of it. The tunes were playing from the music cabinet, there was no measure being used now and it really started to show on both of us. It was a great session, even better than the crack we were having back at the bar (except there was no pool). I was starting to gaze off into space and realised I didn't recognise the musicians that were playing in the last few songs. I tried to look at the music cabinet as if that would change the songs and when I turned back around, there was Kelvin in his birthday suit. All his morning glory, a gun in one hand and his weapon in the other? I was confused, but that didn't last long. 'Now see here, you have drank my nice bottle of fine bourbon and I plan to get something in return,' he said with a grin. 'The way I see it, you either take a shot from this (the gun in his hand) or a shot from this (what he had in his other hand).'"

The Departures Lounge lads were silent. This was the part in the story where Tommy needed a sidekick to properly tell the story and this time it was Dave who obliged.

"I knew that was going to happen," said Dave.

"Well, why didn't you tell Tommy earlier," said Sharkey with a sneer.

Dave cut back in. "So, what did you do?"

There was a long, protracted silence and Tommy roared out, "I'm still here, aren't I?" The howls of laughter reverberated around the pub and one or two of the Departures lads had forgotten they had leaky bladders until it got cold.

III. UNMASKING A MURDERER

There was no hiding it now. The jeans just don't fit her anymore. They never really did. she just beat herself into them. Wiggled and pulled them by the belt loops – those were real handy – wiggled, jumped, and finally closed the button. Job done. This was an exercise that had to be carried out in front of a mirror. The jeans were taken off and for now it was stretchy leggings. Sure, she could fancy them up a bit by wearing a big belt or a nice top, but a t-shirt would do for now. "Have a nice day" was printed on the front of the shirt and she thought to herself today would be a nice quiet day, as she had noting particular to do that day. How wrong a person could be was about to be revealed.

The morning came and went with nothing more exciting than a passing shower of hail, by now it was some time after one o clock and before two. "Better get some lunch," she thought as her belly rumbled. Some fresh flowery soft rolls would be nice.

"Ma, I'm going shops. Need some fresh fish for your dinner?"

"That'll be nice, luv," came the reply.

Vicky grabbed a shopping bag or two. "Better to have it than to look for it," her Gran used to say. What's the harm of an extra bag or two, we've all seen people (especially the lads) getting sent into them European shops for a dozen eggs and bread and coming out with a cango hammer (and no eggs). The local supermarket had all the best fresh stuff. She used to work there at the deli, cutting the meat, filling up the coleslaw, and icing down the best of fish. She knew everyone in the shop and talked to them all, but only liked a few of them.

"Heya, Vera," she said. Vera was one of the older women who worked there. She was always nice to her and really down to Earth. She wasn't in charge of anything, but that didn't stop her thinking that she was and so acted like she ran the place. Vera was very skilled with a filleting knife, she could fillet a stickleback and had more skill with a knife than some surgeons in Dublin.

"What can I get ya, luv?" Vera said.

"I'll have that nice piece of smoked cod; the tail end, please," she said. (This guaranteed no bones, as her ma loved fish but hated bones.) "Thanks V, I'll see ya later." Vicky went to get her fresh rolls and a few bits that were needed, then went along the tills talking to the girls and by a quick scan of the papers headlines (even though they were upside down) she could see some scum had paid the piper the ultimate price. She wondered what luxury goods he traded for with his life. Maybe a few poxy watches and designer clothes, none of which were any use for where he was going now. His poor Ma, having to bury a child, it doesn't bear thinking about. The ground would swallow up his body and all his selfish ways too – live by the sword and die by the sword.

The key turned in the lock and the door opened and into her hallway she flowed, bags hanging from her arms. Struggling to put all the bags onto the table, she thought she should have left some at the door, but then she would have to walk back and get them. It made sense to her to try kill herself by carrying too much shopping; surely everyone did it. She stuck on the kettle and started to put away the messages, most of which she didn't originally go for.

The kettle was at a screeching boil when she noticed a shadow at the front door. She didn't wait for a knock as she had shouted, "I'm coming."

"Who is it?" cried her ma from upstairs.

"I might be psychic, but I'm not a mind reader," she

called back up the stairs. It turned out it was her friend Siobhan (friend in the loosest sense of the word, she didn't have to tell her ma who it was as she had heard Siobhan's big mouth). She could hear her ma muttering to herself, "No good will ever come of that one; she's a nosey cow." Her ma always said that she only came around here for information, not that we ever gave her anything. Re-boiling the kettle, Vicky switched on the radio that was nearby.

"Tea, Siobhan?"

"Yeah," she said. "Half a sugar and a drop of milk." Siobhan was looking around the place. She was always trying to lose weight. Her ma always said, "that one will never lose weight; as curiosity killed the cat, information made her fat." Her ma took this literally to mean the more she gossiped the fatter she got. The radio was playing a good song. She always liked this DJ; even though he had been on the radio for years, he still had his finger on the pulse. Vicky thought for a split second about his poor wife who had passed over.

Siobhan regurgitated some vile gossip about lots of different people. Vicky wondered what it must be like to be perfect. She let the gossip slide and didn't entertain it at all, she focused on her half-eaten

Harry sandwich (for years her ma had worked in a butcher shop on Moore St for a nice butcher named Harry, who her ma was very fond of, and he loved ham, cheese, and mustard sandwiches, which then got the name of a Harry sandwich). It was all over the news about the young lad getting whacked in a drive-by shooting, which she thought was the cowards way as anyone could do that. If, of course, you had sold your soul to the Devil. Siobhan got on her soapbox about the killing and asked, "What do you think? Who done it?" She waited with her eyes and mouth wide open. Vicky stood up to make tea for her ma and looked out the window. She didn't know why she done this, but she looked out of the window while she was washing a cup.

She felt it before she saw the fat little robin hopping along the small wall in the back garden; it had a spirit message with it. "Darren Delaney," she was told killed that young lad from the back of the motorbike. The feelings she got were not nice at all, she might as well have been there as it was such a clear picture.

"Darren Delaney," repeated Siobhan, her eyes wild.

"Oh, fuck," she said. "Did I say that?"

"Yeah, ya did," said Siobhan. "So Delaney is the murderer; I knew he was in a gang."

"Yeah, Darren Delaney shot that young lad. He was the pillion passenger on the motor bike."

Siobhan looked like all of her Christmases had come at once; the mouth of the south was going to tell everyone. This was the juiciest bit of gossip she had ever got and she was going to tell the world – one person at a time.

There was no way she could try to trick Siobhan into thinking she was joking or wrong; Siobhan knew that everything that she said was gospel, a hundred percent legit. Her arse was halfway off the chair and she was gone down the hall before Vicky had the tea for her ma made. "Shit," she thought. "What am I going to do?" There was no taking it back now, the horse had bolted in all sense of the phrase. Siobhan now knew who pulled the trigger and if she could find out who the driver was then she would have the whole story. This story to a Dublin journalist would be front page news, depending on what other news stories it was up against, but it was definitely worthy of the front page.

To Siobhan, this was a way for her to get a fleeting

second of fame with her friends, which she had lots of.

"Is she gone?" her ma asked, knowing full well Siobhan had gone as she had heard her elephantine stomps going up the garden path (in reality elephants are really silent, according to Mr Attenborough).

A ten minute chat was called for on the bed with the Guru. Begrudging every step of the way up that stairs, she walked slowly and silently to converse with her ma who she already knew was right even before anything started.

IV. INTO HIDING/KEBABS

The plan was to get out of the country as fast as possible, but avoiding the normal routes that, though the fastest, would be an easy target. She would be travelling alone; this was the first part of Tommy's plan.

The second part was to put the word out on the street that his niece had fled the country. This would spread far and wide by all the best means possible, by all her family and all the girls in the local shops, on the street corners too, last of all onto the crime network by The Gardai (this was more than likely the Sergeant's idea who drank in the same pub as Tommy). One of the best and fastest ways of spreading news was to tell Siobhan, the gossip queen.

The third part of the plan was to get the family and friends to camp outside his sister's house night and day. The lads volunteered, Dave, Sharkey, Joey and lots of others. The lads just thought of it as being in the pub and really enjoyed doing it.

The nicest of the two suitcases had a broken handle.

It wasn't noticeable until the case was righted onto its wheels. "Why do I keep such rubbish," she thought to herself. "It looks like I will have to repack everything now." This was not done as carefully as the first time. The case looked like it was the same size as the broken one, but it held a lot more inside and lucky enough it could fit more stretchy clothes, which would be needed very soon judging by the size of things.

"Ma, will I need headache tablets?"

"Bring two; they're cheaper over there," said her ma.

Word had got back to the Vera about the goings on at Siobhan's house and now they all knew for real that Darren Delaney was after her. Siobhan's house had been totally thrashed; they broke all the windows in the front of the house and wrote RAT on the path outside her door and threw the rest of the paint everywhere. They also killed her dog and left a note – YOUR FRIEND THE WITCH WILL BE NEXT. Siobhan never thought that telling her little brother's friends the story of the murderer would come back on her so bad. Her little brother was staying put in the house, he was eighteen so old enough to make his own mind up. Her ma was staying too, as she said herself, "Sure where would I go?" The last straw for Siobhan was when they burned her car in broad daylight in the car park. She took what she had on her and fled.

The escape plan was hatched by her ma, her Uncle Tommy, and Vera from the Deli, who was some sort of relation to her ma. This made sense as to why she had always looked upon Vera as an aunty. It now makes sense why Aunty Vera bought her a separate present from the girls on the Deli.

"Ma, which coat should I wear? The long black one or the blue one?" she asked.

"Black; it's a better coat." What she really meant was that *I bought you that black coat for Christmas.* A black taxi pulled up outside the house and beeped. The torrents of tears that flowed in the next few precious moments were a drop in the ocean compared to the volcano of unexpressed emotions erupting between Vicky and her mother. While the driver placed her case in the boot, the lads in the garden said goodbye, and the last she saw of her mother was her face looking out the bedroom window. Dropping her head to stare at the black carpet on the floor of the taxi, her tears fell onto her black coat – the one her ma bought her for

Christmas.

The journey to the train station was very fast. She wanted it to be longer, maybe because she wasn't in a hurry and that's why this part of the journey flew. The papers' headlines in the train station read, GARDA FOLLOWING POSITIVE LEAD IN SHOOTING. She looked away from the headlines real fast as if they were watching her.

Dragging the suitcase up the stairs of the station since the lift was broken, she was glad she had taken a few pairs of jeans out of the case as they would only fit her for a few weeks anyway. She sat on a seat near a broken vending machine, which did not bother her as she wasn't hungry. Her heart was in her mouth and she felt queasy. A big, noisy train went by after a short while. It rolled by slowly and she could see the passengers; it wasn't packed and most of them were looking out the windows and she wondered were any of them going off on a new life like she was.

Her train came shortly after and she picked a window seat facing the direction the train was travelling. She felt sick enough and didn't want to travel in the wrong direction; she didn't like travelling backwards. A shroud of nervous exhaustion settled over her body; this was anxiety hell for her and she told herself not to panic and that this is delayed shock from being forcibly separated from her Ma – she had remembered reading about delayed shock in a book once. The train cleaved its way through the countryside at great speed. Her life was ticking by with the lulling motion of the train.

Something was wrong; the smoke was thick and she was standing barefoot in the street, she did not recognise this place but when the smoke cleared she made out a familiar house. Siobhan screamed out of her broken bedroom window with the white net curtains billowing out into the wind, adding to the horror of the scene. The house was on fire and Siobhan fell out of the bedroom window tangled in the net curtains.

A jerk of the train woke Vicky up, raising her hand to wipe the slobbers from the corner of her mouth. She looked around to see was anyone looking at her. It took her a minute or two to get her bearings. The train had crossed over into the north of Ireland, with only a few stops left in this part of the journey when she would take the ferry from Belfast.

The boat to Scotland was old but comfortable and the staff were very friendly. Her suitcase had gone onto the carousel like in the airport and down into the hold, so at least she didn't have to lug that around as she now only had her small bag to carry.

The tea and fish and chips were really lovely, with a stack of salt and vinegar. She was expecting it all to be shite and really delighted that it wasn't. Soon enough, the port of Stranraer bloomed on the horizon. The taxis were all waiting in the rank when she disembarked from the boat. There were loads of them like she was told there would be.

Always with a smile on her face, Rachel had an outlook on life that would give an Indian swami a run for his money. Nothing seemed to be able to remove the smile from her face, and she was always laughing. It wasn't that she didn't have her share of worries or problems – she had more than some and less than others. Her husband had left her for an older woman. She didn't see this as a problem but more of a miracle since he was a prick, which was why at work they all gave her stick saying, "She must be shit in bed." People at work were like that. They kinda felt sorry for you so they made you feel better by slagging you all the time about the most hurtful of stuff, as if they were doing you a favour by airing your dirty laundry in public. Rachel was no frills kind of girl. This doesn't mean that she didn't like fancy stuff. No, not at all, she did like it. She just didn't have to have it all the time. She liked to do herself up and when she did she felt better and looked good. She wouldn't class herself as being gorgeous, but when she was dolled up she didn't frighten as many people (as one of the pricks at work had said to her).

Now, part of Rachels stress relief system was drink and she could certainly put them away. Beer, spirits, or whatever, it didn't matter as long as there was alcohol in it. That was the plan for tonight. She would go out with one of the girls tonight (Rachel liked to work the bars in small packs, as she had a better chance of snaring a victim) who she knew would be wrapped up back in bed by eleven thirty. So the plan was to bring her friend, Sarah, to the pub and go on to the disco by herself. Sarah was a slightly slimmer model than Rachel, but could not eat or drink as much. Sarah had her own style and was comfortable with it; she was kind of a new age hippie type but not over the top about it, as she liked to describe herself.

A short taxi ride from Rachel's house and they were soon in the centre of town. This was going to be a grand night out as it wasn't too busy but not dead either. Rachel farted nearly on top of Sarah getting out of the taxi, who was lucky she was paying for the taxi. Rachel fell up the kerb laughing, "It's not my fault, it's all that bending over getting out of them taxis."

"I'm glad you are wearing that leather mini, cause I was nearly right behind you, in a cloud of beans," Sarah said. This slagging set the tone for the night and the slagging got better as the shots went down. The drinks they had at Rachel's were now taking effect on Sarah. "One more drink and I'm off," said Sarah, slurring her words a bit.

"Yeah, no problem at all, you get your usual taxi lad and I'll head on inside," said Rachel in eager anticipation.

Rachel knew the bouncer and knew where his birthmark was, so she got in for free. Thirty or so people in the Disco so far, most of them were at the bar so she had the pick of the prime spots. She was going to get a good seat where the girls she knew would stop and chat, so she wouldn't look like a loner there on her own. This was also part of her modus operandi, the lads who were standing near her would say, "Who's your friend?", often to be told to "Fuck right off" by the passing friend. After the chat and on her way to the toilets, Rachel would say to the poor lad, "Don't mind her she hates men" and this usually got the response of "Do you like men?" Rachel would laugh and reel them drinks in, supplied by the lads. A perfect night out. Well, nearly, but it was heading that way.

Rachel's other pressure relief valve was sex. The lads who were currently buying her drinks were fifteen pinters, and she was only at around twelve pints at the moment (she doesn't count the shots) so the lads were ruled out. A quick exit to her left and a two minute walk placed her right outside the drunk's cuisine of choice, kebabs. She had no intention of paying for a kebab herself.

This was going to take military planning and timing. A few minutes of waiting outside stalking the place, she picked her out a perfect victim. She had done this loads of times before and it had always worked – this wasn't her first rodeo. Her target had been acquired, a lone male mouldy from the drink and his feet told her all she needed to know. As he held onto the counter, his feet took two steps forward and one step back, which made his knees buckle and he held onto the counter for dear life; he was prime prey. The funny coincidence was female leopards did this in the wild. She was wearing a leopard print top and they said a leopard never changed its spots. The timing was now, into the kebab house the leopard print top sprang.

"A large doner kebab, extra sauce, with everything on it. Thanks," says Rachel. She knew someone in the next ten minutes would be getting extra sauce. Mr Wobbly's knees stumbled out of the kebab house. While every movement he made was being watched, he took three steps past the end of the building to where Rachel knew there was a dark alley. Out the door she sprinted. Mr Wobbly had only enough time for two small bites from the large kebab before Rachel interrupted.

"Hey, Gary," said Rachel to him while corralling him into the alley and pushing his back up against the wall. Straight in, no kissing, she plunged her hand straight down the front of his jeans while the other hand took his large kebab and put it onto the high windowsill behind him. Then, she dropped to the pavement and took him in her mouth. He was still chewing the kebab and nearly chocked on the bit of kebab in his mouth, but he managed to swallow just before she did. She got up off her knees and walked away. She heard him mumble something behind her, but she just stuck up her hand for the taxi going by. She knew the driver all too well, so it

was okay to make a mess on the back seat like she
had done before.

V. MANCHESTER-REUNITED

Her ma had arranged for her to stay with her aunty
Doris. A fine, homely woman in her later years, she
was a good cook and a baker and her ma's older
sister. Opening the gate she heard a bark. Doris had
a dog. She had seen the dog in the front window, it
looked part Jack Russell and whatever the fuck was
desperate enough to get up on a Jack Russell.

"Come on in," said her aunty Doris, the yoke that
was barking out the window came to have a look
too. "At least it was friendly, probably like its
owner," she thought. Even in these desperate times
she had to laugh. The kettle was put straight on and
the suitcase was put in the guest room. Hugs were
the order of the day, as they had not seen each in
other in quite a while, and too much food was
provided but it was all homemade. It's as if her aunty
had tried to bake away all the troubles. She had
never tried Welsh cakes before and thought them to
be a cross between a scone and a biscuit. The fat,
little dog kept the floor clear of crumbs. An eating
machine, it was, hoovering up raisins, crumbs, and
everything, never to be seen again.

"You must be tired from travelling here the long way, so you can off up for some rest whenever you want. There are fresh sheets on the bed," said her aunty Doris. She had barely taken a breath from saying all that real fast when she said, "Goodnight, love. We can talk tomorrow."

The bed was springy and creaky, but it was warm and smelled of freshly washed sheets. She was glad she was here safe, so she thanked her guides and spirits and then closed her eyes.

An unfamiliar sound woke her in the morning. It sounded like a milk cart, the noise of the empty bottles echoed off the red brick houses. The nice smell of toast wafted down the hallway. She could see her aunty flying around kitchen from press to sink and back again. Vicky moved slowly into the kitchen as not to scare her aunty.

"Come on in, Vicky love. Help yourself, there's fruit juice there. It would be good for the baby," said her aunty Doris while pouring out the tea.

For the next few weeks, time passed with the two of them in a loving bubble and a deep bond of love had developed between them. It had nearly erased the pain that Aunty Doris had felt when she had lost a child all them years ago. The baby was stillborn, a baby boy. Dean, they had called him, and born two days before Vicky.

Lying on her bed on a very windy day, she was thinking that Aunty Doris had the life here. Her husband had passed from a severe asthma attack a few years back, which left all involved in the death feeling very helpless – a useless type of a feeling that did nobody any good. Her aunty was great crack, a head case as they say back home. At that moment Vicky just wanted to hug her ma so tight that she mimicked the action, but all she got was fresh air.

At these moments when the heart was heaviest, the spirits of our loved ones came in really strong. The first few tingles flowed down her body. There were spirits present; she could sense a female spirit that was standing back as such. It was a minder spirit and it was minding Doris's son, Dean, as he played on the floor. This was the strangeness that sometimes happened in the other world. Dean had been stillborn, but he perceived himself as a toddler in a blue Babygro. It reminded Vicky that she needed to buy her own baby clothes – pink ones. She sat there and watched the child play. He smiled at her, this sent a lightning bolt of love right through her whole body. She knew the child wanted her there and his mother needed it. She also sensed her uncle. He wasn't communicating as such, he was just standing there, smiling and glowing with love while minding his son and vice versa.

The noise of the hall door opening brought her back to Earth. It was a gentle experience. It was her aunty, back from the shops again. The shops were a ruse as Aunty Doris was keeping an ear to the ground for any strangers through the oul wan network. The three fastest forms of communication were well known – telegram, telephone, and tell a woman. Anyway all was quiet on the western front. If a dog barked or a bin lid fell, Aunty Doris would be first to know. After all, you didn't spend half a century living in an area and making lots of friends and not be able to call in a few favours. Vicky went back to her uncle's spirit, an instantaneous connection of souls. She realised that aunty Doris had felt responsible all these years for Dean's death. Vicky decided that Aunty Doris could say, "it's good for the baby" a million more times if it helped her to heal.

VI. THE COALMAN DELIVERS

Sharkey worked one or two days a week for a mate of his in the fuel business. At this time of the year, as the orders were slackening off due to the weather, it was just a day here and there making deliveries in the lorry. This was the time to gather, stack, cut, and chop wood, or lumber as it was known in the business. It was stacked as high as the roof, it would take months to bag all of that.

Today, they were going out doing a few deliveries. A handy job since he didn't have to drive the big lorry; all he had to do was sit there and lump the stuff into peoples' sheds. His mate since primary school, Joey, did the driving.

"Where do you want to go for a bit of lunch?" asked Joey.

"Well, I'll tell ya what, I don't want to go to that new fancy sandwich place," said Sharkey. "The place at the end of the town, as I heard a lad got a ham and yeti's cheese bap and paid a bleedin' fortune for it."

"Fuck that," said Joey. "I don't want to have to getta mortgage out to have lunch. I know where we'll go." The local greasy spoon was the perfect spot; a good feed that didn't require a loan from the money lenders. During the lunch they sat in the furthest corner from people, kinda out of ear shot of the other punters.

"Hi luv, I'll start off with two mugs of tea. The usual, Joey?" the waitress said as she stopped by the table.

"I'll have the same and chips as well, and a refill when you're coming back, thanks," Sharkey said (he wasn't paying and he was a little bit mean, so was going to fill up). She brought two full Irish and was turning away when Sharkey said with a mouthful of sausage visible to the world, "Where's me chips?"

"Don't get your knickers in a twist, they're comin, I've only one pair of hands," she said, scolding him like a bold child. The chips came out when it was too late to enjoy them with the fry up. Sharkey thought she did that on purpose; he had wanted to dip his chips in his egg and beans like a spoiled child.

The third mug of tea was now on the go. Joey started off with a story.

"Did I ever tell ya about the time me and the wife were driving home through The Glen of The Downs and I knocked down a small animal?"

"No," said Sharkey, trying to muffle the heat out of a scalding chip.

"Yeah, I knocked it down, as I said, and she screamed in the van when I swerved. We got out to have a look at what it was and if it was alright. Wouldn't fuckin believe me when I tell ya, but it was a skunk and it was still alive. My wife asked what we were going to do. I said, 'I know, I read it somewhere in a book, on what to do in such situations, ya have to keep it quiet, in the dark and warm.' Then she reminded me that the heating is still fuckin' broke. So I told her to stick it down her knickers. And she said, "You can fuck right off with yourself. And what about the smell?' So I said 'Ah, sure fuck it. If it dies, it dies.'"

Sharkey's laugh is startled out of him so the chip in his mouth was already half way across the table, fuelled by him chocking on it, and the tea was streaming down both nostrils mixed in with snots. A two minute clean-up was called for with all available hankies.

"Come on, daylights burning," said Joey as he shuffled out of the booth (followed by a good scratch and sniff). A quick trip to the jacks was called for and then back into the lorry that was all ready to go. A few more deliveries made as the day went by, the only excitement was getting chased by a mad dog.

"We only have two more deliveries," said Joey with a wry smile on his face. They got to the last order in the early evening. Sharkey knew this house well and he also knew what happened next. Joey would bring the coal in by himself and take about half an hour to come back out, since this was Mrs Whites house. Joey always said when he got here, "Once you go black, you never go back." Sharkey knew he would have to wait around, as Joey did this one himself, so he just sat there re-reading the paper and thinking about the swimming he had done with the lads in The Forty Foot during the last week and reminded himself to return the key to the swimmers hut.

The other lad wasn't long at all and he pulled himself up into the lorry by the handle. They only had a short ten minute drive to get home. Sharkey looked at the other lads ruffled hair. It was then he noticed his hand, the two middle fingers on Joey's left hand were cleaner than the rest. "Fuck me," thought Sharkey, "Poor Mrs White." As they were pulling up outside Sharkey's house, Joey's clean hand rummaged in his pocket, for a few pound for Sharkey for helping him and he gave it to him.

"I am pulling a bit of timber out of a bad spot next week. I'll drop by on Tuesday morning at the usual time and get you. See you then, Sharkey," said Joey. He drove off up the road in a plume of blue diesel smoke and was gone. Sharkey stuck the money deep down into his pocket and opened the hall door, the smell of frying onions filled the place with their smell.

"Heya. Burgers, onions, and mash," said his wife.

"I'm just going to have a quick wash first. Did ya put on the emersion heater like I asked y–" He never got to finish that sentence as the gravy splashed a little bit on her hand.

"Of course I put the poxy fuckin water on. Isn't there hot water? Where do ya think that came from? Next door? Ya fuckin clown."

"Jaysus, I only asked," Sharkey said like a scalded cat while washing his fingers. He thought of Joey the slut, as he calls himself. "Half of the women around here I have kept warm, and all the others I've sold coal," Joey always said. Dinner was uneventful, except that one of his twin girls had earlier fallen off a bike, which he thought was strange as she didn't have a bike, but she had cut her knee that had a plaster on it. Plasters fixed nearly everything. Sharkey wondered if they had plasters for marriages and pictured his wife with a big plaster over her mouth. He dared not say it out loud as he wasn't in the mood for losing another row. Sharkey threw the wife a few pounds so she can fuck off out to the Bingo and he would get some well-earned ear rest, as he was going to babysit his own kids and maybe watch a film in peace.

VII. THE FISHING TRIP

It was the early morning of the boat fishing trip; it had finally come and with no time to waste Tommy was out of the bed like a shot. A quick glance out of the opened window confirmed the wind was had died down overnight. There were a few clouds in the sky, but it didn't look like rain. Then on into the bathroom, a quick piddle and shake and then a wash standing at the sink as he had no time for a shower – daylight was burning. A good spray with the oul body deodorant left the bathroom in a haze. A change of vest but the jocks didn't need a change as he had only put them on yesterday. He flew down the stairs to put on the kettle a half a slice of bread into the toaster, butter on toast, tea down the hatch, and he was out the door. He was on his way to do a quick touch up job, no real hard work for him today, none of your nonsense wallpaper patterns today. Oh no, he'd be in and out, done and dusted before eleven AM. This left him plenty of time to go and collect some bait he had ordered during the week and he would also get some prime fishing spots from the seller of the worms. A drop into the fishing gear shop to get some new hooks was also on the cards along with more tips on where to fish.

Sharkey had a good stretch in the bed. Probably a little too good, as he had clawed her calf with his big toenail.

"Ah, ya cunt ya. Your big clawey fuckin' nail," she said in her usual caring tone. She's overreacting, he thought, it's not as if she got hit by a bulldozer; even if she had, the fat cow would probably break it. He didn't dare say this out loud.

"Me bleedin' leg. You and your claws. Would ya not cut them," she moaned.

"Ah, here. Fuck this, I'm off for a swim," he said, mumbling to himself.

Had she heard him? Amazing thing that, he thought, women have supersonic hearing only when you don't want them to hear you.

"I hope you don't cut someone in half with them fuckin nails while you're swimming," she said.

She must have won fuck all at the Bingo, he thought to himself, while he looked at the living expression of eighty-eight, as she was fat enough to be both of the fat ladies. Another extraordinary ability women had, along with their great hearing, was a natural tendency to exaggerate the fuck out of everything when they argued. Sharkey had too much in his head, this was dangerous territory for him. "There's no way I'm getting caught twice in the one morning," he whispered to himself, getting out of bed. The hall door closed behind him. It was a relief, like closing the cage on an angry hippo and he felt safer the more he walked away from her. He took a deep breath and put his rolled-up towel under his arm, thinking that a nice swim would do him a world of good.

He could hear the snores in his bedroom getting louder and louder as the dominant female took over the whole bed.

Thoughtful as always, Dave brought up a cup of tea and a kiss for his wife. He also had tea and toast on the same tray for Romeo along with a drop of fresh orange juice. Dave thought that Romeo might need a bit of re-fuelling as he had a heavy date last night. At least when he went out and met the girls there never seemed to be as many dirty socks under Romeo's bed. Dave actually felt sorry for Romeo's mattress, probably because he was more related to the mattress than he was to Romeo at this point. He laughed when he thought of Romeo trying to turn the mattress into a solid concrete block and the curtains got a rest too. Was he the reincarnation of a sperm whale? As Dave did most of the laundry and housework (he loved it and didn't complain) and all of the gardening. It was no use. Romeo was dead to the world, so he brought the breakfast back down the stairs and he shouted up the stairs to the love of his life, "Would you like more tea, baby?"

"No, thanks," came the reply from his grateful wife. Karen lay in the bed on fresh sheets supplied by Dave as she flicked through a women's fashion magazine. She really loved Dave as they were childhood sweethearts and also that gold top on page four. Flicking another page over, she looked over at the wardrobe at the end of the room. She didn't like it as it was dated. She had always wanted a walk in wardrobe so she could have all her nice clothes hung up instead of folded away in a wardrobe. If they were all hung up she could easier pick what she wanted to wear for that day.

Dave sat down to watch a bit of telly. He had the washing out on the line since earlier this morning. He loved the nature programs with David Attenborough in them and his luck was in today since *The Ants of The Kalahari Desert* was on. He sat there amazed at the telly, imagining how the ants could only spend forty-five seconds on the blistering hot sand before they died from the heat; he imagined that women could only spend forty-five seconds in clothes shops instead of the forty-five minutes he was usually left waiting while his wife finished shopping.

The Three Amigos, as they were known in the pub, met up on the slipway in Bullock Harbour. Tommy was over talking to the crab pot man, probably getting the update on the best fishing spots or places to stay away from. Dave was down looking at the swan. He had been hoping he would not see it, because he thought it brought him bad luck. He never caught anything after seeing the swan. Sharkey was over talking to two older men (they were grave dodgers, Sharkey called them), they were probably swimmers. Sharkey gave them a key; it must have been for the swimmers shed down in the Forty Foot.

Time to go with all their gear, rods, bait, sandwiches, and bucket already loaded into the boat. It was a small boat, but it was big enough for the three of them. It was a fourteen foot boat with a little cabin at the bow and an outdoor motor on the flat end (as the lads in the pub called it). The engine basically sounded like a lawnmower engine and puffed out a bit of blue smoke. It wasn't yet noon and they had cleared the mouth of the harbour. The tide was coming in, so they would have plenty of time to fish before there wasn't enough water to get the boat back and onto the trailer.

Brand new sets of feathers were taken from their packets and tied onto the line on the rod, then a weight was attached and a bit of bait, as simple as that. The feathers were sent down into the deep dark unknown armed with the best of baits. Gulls circled overhead and a gentle breeze was blowing; it was supposed to stay like that all day.

They were out in the really deep water in line with Dalkey Island when the first of the mac-mac came onboard, caught by Dave off all people. Maybe the curse of the swans was broken. They continued on for the next while with only small stuff being caught (no fish big enough to bring home). They caught some nice, big Rock Bream, but they didn't eat those so threw them back in. The Three Amigos didn't really talk much for the first few hours, not that they had taken a vow of silence. It was more like that the gentle lapping of the small waves at the pointy end of the boat were licking away their stress.

"Who the fuck?" The boat wobbled from side to

side; someone was moving around the boat as if they were on dry land. The rule was stay low and move slow. The bucket was grabbed unceremoniously, as it was usually passed along in a line up to the top of the boat, where it was used for number two's.

"Me sandwiches," said Dave as he took his sandwiches out of the bucket. They were only wrapped in bread paper, which was now wet. "I can't eat them now, they're ruined. All wet and soggy."

"What were they, Dave?" asked Sharkey, hoping Dave would take the bait.

He did. "They were ham."

"More like ham and sweetcorn," laughed Sharkey. Tommy was also laughing at the two of them.

The drift into Killiney Bay was always a scenic one. Killiney Bay has been compared to the Bay of Naples in Italy, but without the need for a coat for the cold. The roads around the area reflected this fact, with names like Vico, Sorrento, etc.

The oul engine was pulled back into life and the boat was brought to just a few hundred yards off the beach. Dogs, people, and a few small kids could be seen playing on the beach. The boat was set to drift off shore as the westerly breeze was blowing.

"I usually fish over wrecks with muppets and now the wrecks and muppets are in the boat," Tommy laughed as he jigged his feathers. All he got from the other two was a smirky smile. The boat drifted further from the beach and any minute now they would be into to some nice fish. They were covering some nice ground (that could hold fish); the possibility of a nice fish was definitely on the cards. Tommy's rod was the first to bend. He struck, setting the hook into the fish as it dived. Tommy reeled back in the line and it dived again.

"Pollock," shouted Sharkey as the fish broke surface. It was a nice size fish, even if it had a very bland flavour. He dispatched the fish with a bang on the noggin and gutted the fish straight away.

Not much else was caught. Tommy said they were drifting too fast, flying over the fish. A small dab and a cod, surrendered to Sharkey's feathers (the lads said the cod had a suicide note). They needed to find better ground if they were going to catch for dinner tomorrow. They were the best part of a mile offshore, no longer could people be seen and only forests and mountains were discernible. A big yellow metal buoy, which is about the size of a house, bobbed in the distance.

"Let's go there," said Sharkey, throwing the dirty bucket down to the flat end of the boat. Sharkey was hoping the move would get him some cod, which he liked to fry up and have with mash. Tommy was a grand driver of the boat, which meant the lads hardly ever got splashed. "We can tie off that yoke, so we don't drift any further," said Sharkey.

"I think this is deep water. I'm not sure if we have enough anchor rope to reach the bottom, and I wouldn't want to be pulling that up from all the way down there," said Tommy. There were lots of jellyfish here, the harmless ones with the purple in them, and a swarm of them were drifting by.

"Oh lovely," said Sharkey. "The mac-mac do be around with them." He recalled some old story that one of the coffin dodgers told him. "Get in real close to the buoy and I'll throw a rope on it." Sharkey stood with a length of rope in his hands.

Bang! Sharkey fell into the boat and the engine conked out, the bow of the boat had crashed into the buoy.

"Who the fuck put that shit bucket there?" Tommy

shouted. The bucket had stopped the tiller handle from making a left turn so the bow of the boat that Sharkey was lying in had crashed into the buoy; it was no joke. Sharkey untangled himself from the rope and, quick as a flash, looked around for damage. Dave was as white as a sheet and was worried looking. Tommy was fuming. Sharkey smiled and said to Tommy, "You wouldn't be related to the captain of the Titanic by any chance, would ya?" Laughter echoed all over the place and the bucket was passed back up to the bow for safety sake.

"Water," said Dave, panicking. He was looking into the bottom of the boat. Dave knew that the boat was repaired a few years ago, with a good crack in the bow. But the water was coming in fast.

"Start up the engine quickly, Tommy," yelled Sharkey.

Tommy was all fingers and thumbs after seeing the water gushing into the boat and the fact that the engine had stalled. Sharkey shouted at Dave to start bailing out the water with the bucket. Dave was doing his best, but it wasn't enough. Sharkey lunged to the back of the boat, grabbed the supply bag with the bait wrapped in newspaper and the last sandwich. He tossed the bait and sandwich out of the bag, grabbed the spare full petrol can, and put a drop of it on the bag with the paper. He went back past the two lads who were working like mad, and standing at the front he lit the bag on fire on top of the little cabin. Dave looked up at Sharkey.

"What?" said Dave, even more nervous than before.

"Tommy, anything out of that engine?" Sharkey asked without even turning to look at Tommy, as he was doing probably the most important job of setting the boat on fire.

"What the fuck are you at?", shouted Tommy.

"We have to try an attract someone's attention for help; them posh people in Killiney have house phones," he said to Tommy, who was now standing up at the back of the boat, looking out to sea. "Keep bailing. Good man, Dave," encouraged Sharkey, while looking into the sea where Dave was bailing the water. The jelly fish were still drifting by, oblivious to the drama around them. A pair of skiddy jocks floated by with the jelly fish. Trying to figure out where the shitty Y-fronts came from, Sharkey looked around and seen the most unexpected thing that he thought he could see –

Tommy's big white arse.

"What the fuck are you at, Tommy?" said Sharkey, shocked.

"I'm not having my body washing up on some beach with dirty underpants on," said Tommy half-laughing. By now the water in the boat was up past their ankles and the water was cold. Not knowing how much more weight the boat could take, Sharkey threw everything overboard – the rods, bait and fish, even the anchor. Dave stood up and grabbed Sharkey by his jacket sleeve, with tears in his eyes.

"Tell Karen and the lads I love them, won't you Sharkey?" said Dave. Sharkey nodded slowly as Dave let the jacket go. The last thing that Sharkey could remember was being thrown out of the boat, hitting the sea with his back first, as the boat flipped with the three lads going in different directions. Sharkey came up a gasped a quick breath to see that the boat was gone. It had sunk. He got a terrible feeling in his guts, more for the lads than himself. When he looked to where the boat had been, he saw Tommy and Dave splashing for their lives. Dave could not swim at all and Tommy could only do the width of a pool. Thankfully, both of them had their backs to him. Sharkey was threading water twenty feet from the lads wondering what the fuck he should do as he looked for anything that was floating. There was nothing. "I can't save two, but I have to," he thought. "I can make the beach in two hours, if I take one of them, which one do I take? If I take one at all?"

Dreadful decision to make, he didn't want to be here but he was here. The boat had sunk only about thirty seconds ago by now and time seemed to be at a standstill. "Who do I save? Tommy, as I've known him longer, or Dave who is really sound?" The word *sound* caught in his brain. The sound was less, there wasn't as much splashing as before, Dave had stopped splashing and was floating face down in the water, Sharkey was dumb struck, until Tommy who had turned around now to face him called out. Sharkey was an excellent swimmer and was there in a flash, Tommy grabbed a hold of him with both hands and they went under, when they were under Sharkey used his knee and then his arm to break the hold, it worked and he pulled three breaststrokes underwater away from Tommy. He came up about ten feet from Tommy's splashing around.

"Please, please," gasped and sobbed Tommy. Tommy's head was under the water more now than it was above. Sharkey thought again of trying to save

Tommy, but he was much bigger and stronger and he could pull both of them down. It was then that he decided to save himself. He started to swim slowly away from Tommy and towards the shore; he could hear Tommy crying behind him. It was an awful action to have to take, but there was nothing Sharkey could do. He started to cry, a few more slow strokes and the splashing behind him had stopped. Sharkey turned around to have a look at his dead mates, but that was not what he saw, as the near-empty red petrol tank had risen to the surface. It must have broken off from the petrol line that was attached to the engine and Tommy was hanging onto it. Sharkey flew back to his mate at full speed, stopping five feet away.

"Fuck me, Sharkey, I thought that I was a goner then," said Tommy, bobbing in the water.

"You hang on tight there, Tommy, help is coming. Someone had to have seen that black smoke," said Sharkey. Somebody had. A little old lady in Killiney had seen the smoke and rang the Gardai, who in turn got onto the lifeboat and were at that moment steaming their way to them, in one of the biggest class of rescue boat. Tommy and Sharkey were wrapped in blankets as Dave's body was brought onboard and the Three Amigos were now down to two.

VIII. THE DREAM

Vicky knew that there was something wrong, because she was standing in her mother's room and all of the furniture was missing except for the wardrobe, which stood at the wall opposite the bed. It was making a rattling noise and the doors were bouncing open. She moved closer to it cautiously; she had a feeling something was not right and she was a little bit scared, but moved all the same. Time had slowed down and all sound was gone, that was when she felt it. The feeling came all at once and she knew she was dreaming; she knew she was asleep in her aunty Doris's house and could remember what she had for dinner and she also remembered that she was psychic. She felt a great, almost almighty presence that was there, slowing down time and casting a beautiful blue light. It had an aura of protection around it making her feel and also connected to universal knowledge. Vicky looked upon a beautiful angel; she did not feel worthy to be gazing upon such magnificence. The angel had a blue gown on. It was all hazy around the Angel, as if it stepped through a rift into this world to tell her something really life changing.

The angel spoke (as in it communicated by

smiling and speaking to her and all the questions Vicky wanted to ask were answered in that smile), "Bring this with you my child." The angel pointed to what looked like an old red petrol can on the floor. "You are worthy my child, as are all good souls. You carry a boy child and you may call your little angel Dean." With that the Angel was gone. Vicky was thinking of Aunty June. She was such a messer that even in death she was still at it. In walked her ma. She was really happy to see her as she missed her terrible. Vicky had the red petrol tank in her hands and she could now smell the petrol and feel the remains in it sloshing around.

"Hurry up, Vicky", her mother said while turning to go down the stairs. The wardrobe shook and she opened it this time and looked in. To her surprise, there were no clothes in it, but inside was like an aquarium. She could actually see a small boat sitting on the sea floor, with purple jelly fish swimming by. "What am I to do?" asked Vicky.

"Throw it," said a voice that she recognized. It was her uncle Tommy. So, she did as she was told and she swung that can into that wardrobe as hard as she could and prayed.

Upon waking that morning, Vicky had a tiredness

within her. Not a sleepy tiredness, but one where her energy had been spent and she lay there and took in a few deep breaths. She could hear the milkman in the distance. She stretched her arms toward the ceiling, she got a fright as there were little spots of blood on her hands and she wondered where had it come from. "The baby," she thought and she whipped back the covers down past her feet, but nothing there. She examined her hands after she opened the curtains, and figured it was red nail varnish or paint on her hands. She went to the bathroom and on passing her auntie's bedroom, the door was open and the bed was already made. She knew her aunt was cooking downstairs, as she could smell baking. She hoped it was her brown bread, which was her own recipe; it was to die for and Vicky had never tasted better. She spied her aunt's wardrobe and her dream came flooding back and she remembered the angel telling her she was having a boy. "A boy," she laughed. "Dean."

Down the stairs she went with an unnatural love in her heart for this yet unborn child, sitting sideways now at the kitchen table since the bump was getting too big to eat over – she didn't like dropping food all over the baby and the floor, not that the dog minded. Even though she felt tired, she had a buzz about her that her aunty picked up on.

"Will ya have a try of these sausages?" said aunty Doris while bending over the grill.

"The sausages aren't the same over here," said Vicky.

"I wouldn't say so, love," said her aunty, laughing. Vicky drank down her tea and thought about how the tea was different too; it must be the water with all the lime scale in it. The kettle was be full of it and they had none of that stuff in Dublin. She decided to tell her aunty about the dream she had last night. She started off slowly as she didn't want to spook her aunty, after all this was her home. "I had a dream or a vision last night," she said. It was Sunday morning now and, even though she didn't work, Vicky still liked the calmness and the pace of relaxing and enjoying her breakfast.

"Yeah, any good looking fella's in it for me," said Aunty Doris with half of a sliced pan of toast in her hands.

"It was very strange; I was back in my ma's house," said Vicky.

"That'll be wanting to have the baby back home,"

says her aunty, with a slight sadness in her voice while running her fingers under the tap.

"It was more than that," said Vicky.

Now Irish people tended to do this, as in you didn't stop the flow of the story in order to correct the other person; it was as if the story had more precedence than the people telling it. Most just go "yeah, yeah" and let the story move on, even if they were nearly sure that the storyteller was wrong.

"I'll just have to blurt it out," thought Vicky, as her aunty took her seat again and poured out the tea. "I seen an angel, me ma and Tommy were there, too,' said Vicky, half-guessing the response, she was wrong.

"Well, you're not the first in this family to see an angel. Your ma was told by one to call you Victoria, but your ma decided that was too old fashioned so she calls you Vicky." said her aunty Doris with a smile on her face. She thought the rest of the dream too weird to tell her aunty, so she left it at that and had some more toast.

On Monday mornings, her aunty went to the shops at around ten o clock. While she was out she also collected her pension and brought home some shopping.

Vicky ran a bath and put some relaxing stuff into the water. The baby liked the bath and she could see his foot sticking out her belly. She was lying back soaking all the time away and she must have dozed off for a good while, as when she woke her hands were wrinkly and the bath water was only warm. She got herself out of the bath and started to dry herself when her aunty barged through the bathroom door, frightening her.

"Me fanny," she shouted as she grabbed for the nearest thing – her dressing gown.

"You may as well lie in the nip in the middle of O'Connell Street, as you better get used to people staring at your bits," said her aunty. "When your decent come down to me, I have news for you, love."

She dressed as quick as she could, but with all the powder and lotion she has to put on she took longer than she expected. By the time she got to the kitchen table, her tea that was poured for her was barely warm.

"Looks like you are going home", said her aunty, with sadness in her voice.

"What do you mean?" replied Vicky.

"It's your uncle, Tommy," said her aunty. Strange emotions and feelings were whirring around in Vicky's guts. She thought she was going to be sick, so she got up to go to the toilet and noticed there was blood on her chair; her aunty had seen it too and moved in real fast and caught Vicky before she fell. She put her back in her chair. When she was safely sitting down, her aunty picked up the phone and called Paddy, a very short while later a knock came at the door. "Royal Victoria Hospital, Paddy as quick as you can," said her aunty quickly. Vicky thought that the baby's head was coming as she could only really walk sideways like a crab. It was difficult to get into the cab and sitting in the back seat, she thought it was too early for the baby to be born. Paddy was a really fast driver and he had them at the entrance of the hospital in no time. Her aunt flew into the emergency ward and came back with not one but two nurses and a wheelchair, they put her into it. So she sat back and let the nurses do their bit. "Them nurses will take good care of you," said her aunty as she was telling them nurses that Vicky was her niece.

Her aunty Doris was pacing like mad, marching up and down as if she was having the baby herself.

Four minutes had gone by and she marched out the door and it wasn't very long when she came back with a doctor. The doctor did a full examination; Vicky was mortified.

"You are in labour, about two centimetres dilated. It's a little early for baby to be born."

Quick as a flash, her aunty Doris interrupted. "Doctor Mustafa, a word please." Her aunty moved in and corralled the Doctor away from the bed. All that Vicky overheard was the doctor saying, "The development of the baby's lungs are a concern, we need to stop the labour." Aunty Doris bounded back beside the bed as the Doctor went to talk to the nurse.

"The doctor said you will be grand now; they will put you on a drip." Vicky never heard the doctor saying that and wondered if her aunty was spinnin' a yarn. She was brought straight up to the ward and put on a drip. She put two and two together and realised something similar must have happened her aunty when her baby was stillborn. The nurse that put in the drip in was really young, around her age, and she told her that the drip had "fanny closing medicine in it".

The bleeding continued for the rest of that day, but when she woke in the morning it had stopped.

They sent her back home the next day with tablets to take for the next four days. Her poor auntie's back must have been broke from sleeping in a chair. The doctor told her to go straight to her GP or Clinic when she got home to Dublin and her aunty Doris told her that they would not be going to Dublin for a few days until they both had a rest, and that the drug to stop the baby coming would more than likely be taken off her in Ireland. The word that her aunty got back from Dublin was that Darren Delany's gang got caught red-handed with a shit load of drugs. She also told her uncle Tommy was the main reason they all got caught and the sergeant in the bar got a promotion.

IX. HOMEWARD BOUND

All the papers in the train station were covering the story about the gang back home all getting arrested. They were all going to be done for murder, and since they were part of a gang, they would not be seen for a very long time. Anyone loosely connected to the gang had either gone to ground or fled the country. There was an Irish Army presence at the courts, considering the crime and the nature of the gang. On the opening day of the trail, the judge stated that this type of heinous crime would not be tolerated in Irish society and needed a strict response. Vicky was going to be taking the direct route home this time and she wasn't returning alone. Her favourite aunty Doris was with her. (Her aunt had dropped off the carpet cleaner with her friends so it could be minded; hopefully he will be slimmer when she gets back.) Her aunt knew this travel route as she had taken it before, but not recently enough for her liking. Her aunty knew all she had to do was keep Vicky calm and hydrated, they would be getting trains from Manchester to Crewe and then Crewe to Holyhead (Liverpool to Dublin was on strike and she didn't like to set foot in Liverpool).

"Here you go Vicky, love," she said, handing her the

tea and custard creams. "Do you know what drives me mad? It's the prices these places charge. I could have bought the whole pack for the same price in the shop." Her aunty Doris stirred her tea and shook her head.

"Aunty Doris," said Vicky. Her aunty paid one hundred percent attention to her, wondering what was so important and what was coming next. (When Dubliners used the full name or title, something was up). Before Vicky could tell her aunty Doris what she had on her mind, a big hairy rocker fella sat right down next to Vicky. He had big leather boots and a jacket with badges, he was blasting *Bohemian Rapsody* by Queen on the wireless (as aunty Doris called it) and he was drinking cans of cider. Another heavy rock song was next on his playlist, one she didn't recognise, and aunty did not like judging by the face on her.

The train was coming and they got a grand seat near the back of the carriage. Vicky felt a presence,. It was Aunty June. She said, "You won't be going anywhere for a while, but you will get home safe tonight." Then, she was gone. Vicky told her aunty Doris what had just happened and the message as well.

"It's nice to know they walk with us and go on

trains, too," her aunty said with a laugh. A minute or two later, an announcement came over the speakers, "We are sorry to announce that this train will not be leaving the station until further notice."

"Well, I'm off to the shop for a magazine or two. Do you need anything?" said Vicky as she wobbled out of the seat and table.

"No, love. I'm grand, I'm going to just shut my eyes for forty winks," said aunty Doris as she closed her eyes. Vicky got off the train, when she was half way to the shop, she turned to look at her aunty asleep. She wasn't. In fact, her aunty was like an Alsatian on steroids, her eyes following her every step. Vicky just smiled and carried on into the shop thinking about how her very own guardian angel was sitting on a train going nowhere.

The speaker squeaked back to life. "We have just been informed the delay is a grass fire; we will keep you updated", said the announcement. Vicky picked up two magazines and a roll of minty sweets. She rooted in her bag for her money and thought, "I must clean this out." When she took her head out of the bag her aunty was right there.

"Fuckin Jasus, you frightened me," said Vicky.

Another announcement stated the train would be leaving in five minutes. They were back on the train in a flash (with aunty holding Vicky's arm). They only had to wait another four minutes and forty three seconds before departing the station. She might be old, but she sure can move when she wants too. It wasn't long until they could smell the grass smoke, then they could see parts of a blackened field and a yellow fire brigade was spraying out water.

Boarding the boat, Vicky followed her aunty. This guaranteed them the best seats on the boat (her aunty was like a sniffer dog, not for contraband, but for good seats). Surprisingly, they got great seats for their return to Dublin. Both of them had a light nap on the sofa. Aunty Doris stayed awake when Vicky was asleep, looking at faces on that boat. A good neighbour of her ma's was waiting when they got off of the boat. Frank was an ex-driver for a taxi company. He knew all the short cuts. Everybody liked Frank, he loved to drive, chat, and was always smiling and wearing his good jacket. As Frank said, "there's two types of bad driver's, oul wan's and oul lads that drive like oul wan's." Her ma was waiting for her with the hall door opened. She could not remember the last time her ma was downstairs it must have been years ago. Bags and suitcases were brought in by Frank, while the three women got into one big hug. Her ma gave lovely hugs. The first pot of tea of many was on the brew. Vicky was making it.

"Any news, Ma?" asked Vicky.

The two sisters looked at each other. "Listen, love," said Doris.

Her ma took over. "We didn't want to upset you in your condition." The competition for best storyteller had begun; her ma had won the hugging competition.

"It's Dave, Vicky love. He had a heart attack while he was out fishing with your uncle; they are lucky to be alive." said her ma.

"Tommy's Dave?"

"Yes, love," said Doris. At that moment, Vicky wondered why she didn't get a message or feel Dave's passing. Maybe her guides knew she had enough on her plate. She was sad, as they were all really close. His poor Karen. They stayed up all night and boiled the bollocks out of the kettle, they had so much talking and catching up to do.

The next morning her ma took to the bed and was

holding court in her room again. When Vicky got up, the sisters were already two pots of tea ahead of her and a plate of toast. They were still talking as she walked in; they must have had a lot to talk about. Vicky got under the covers beside her ma.

"Jasus, you're nearly ready to pop," said her ma.

"Are you having a natural birth or is baby coming out through the sunroof?" laughed her aunty.

"I'm going to have all my essential oils on me to help with the birth," said Vicky. The two women erupted with laughter. "What's so funny?" asked Vicky.

"You'll see," said her ma, wiping the tears from her eyes. "We'll be going to Dave's funeral tomorrow morning, if you feel up to it." The choice did not sound great to her – stay here on her own or show up at the funeral where everyone would ask a million questions about the murder and the baby and going into hiding. She decided to ask her guides what to do, as she trusted they would always look after her.

X. THE FUNERAL

The morning had come and the two sisters had been up since cock crow A light fry up was waiting for Vicky when she ventured into the kitchen where her ma was doing the cooking! One egg, one rasher, one sausage, and a slice of toast, washed down by a nice mug of tea and a drop of orange juice (for the baby), and the women were ready. There was a knock on the door. It was their lift to the funeral. It was a very quiet affair with only a few people crying. This was not a reflection on Dave's character, but everyone was saying that people were still in shock. Her uncle Tommy was not at the funeral, as he was confined to the bed by the doctor as he was in serious shock. The stories had gone around about Tommy in the boat in his Jaye's Fluid. People were laughing at his antics even though he had faced certain death.

Dave's poor wife was beside herself with grief and poor oul Romeo didn't know what to do with himself for once. After the graveyard, everyone was going back to the pub for soup and sandwiches, but Vicky and her ma and Doris were going straight back home. The sisters were talking about making a nice pot of tea as if they had just walked the Sahara Desert.

Her ma made lovely egg and onion sandwiches while Aunty Doris whipped out a nice box of Scottish Shortbreads that she must have bought on the boat. The sandwiches were inhaled along with a lovely drop of tea, a plague of locusts wouldn't have had a patch on the women devouring them sandwiches. The only evidence left was a few crumbs leftover on the plates. In the middle of the feeding frenzy it emerged that uncle Tommy would be coming over when the doctor said he was okay. Dinner was going to be an absolute favourite of hers, a lovely lump of Brisket Corned Beef and savoy cabbage and a fresh apple tart was also getting threatened to be made. Liver, bacon, and onions was tonight's dinner. Vicky wasn't too fond of liver, so she was having an extra few rashers and mash with butter running in rivers through them like yellow lava. The plan was to relax in front of the telly. It really didn't matter what was on the telly, as the talking would ensure that you would not be able to follow a film. So, a quiz show was put on instead and they answered a handful of the questions between them. A nap was called for, drifting off into a warm comfortable sleep to the sounds of the quiz show. Vicky woke with a fright; she had dreamt she was falling.

"Good evening," said aunty Doris. "She's awake now."

"I'll stick the kettle on," said her ma. "Dinner will be about half an hour." So it was nearly to the exact minute that dinner was ready, the table was all laid out by the chefs helper, Aunty Doris. After the dinner, a film was on and the two sisters had cleaned up and prepared the veg for tomorrow. Vicky felt like she was just sleeping and eating, that every day was the same. She had to sit around and wait for time to pass, so she went up to have a bath. Soon, she was all snuggly and wrapped up warm in bed.

The next day had a Christmas type of feel to it (without the presents, tree and decorations, of course). The excitement was in the air as Aunty Doris had not seen here brother in a long while and after what had just happened it brought it all home – family was everything. A nice heavy breakfast of a fry up with all the trimmings, a kind of full Irish/English (with pan fried potato chips), that would stand for them until dinner time.

"It's through your belly that you grow," her gran used to say. Sure you would never know what aunty Doris would pull out of her bag. Dessert was in the cards, too. After the big feed, there were pots back on the cooker. Vicky went upstairs as the smell of food made her feel sick when she was stuffed. She was lying on the bed and reading on of the mags from the train station shop, it was packed with rich celebs in their big posh houses and cars.

An unexpected sleep happened to her and dreams took control of her reality, off and away to a surprise destination not determined by her. She found herself feeling weird as she started her dream in some else's house. She stood on the landing with all the doors opened, and a faint light was coming from the room on her right. Vicky looked at her hands for some reason; maybe she was trying to make sense of what was happening. The light was a strange shade of blue. She looked at the light and remembered that she was dreaming and that she had some control over it, a knowing sense came over her. She knew she was psychic. She went toward the light, on into that room, still not recognising where she was. She was calm and could feel a strong sense of love here, and that made her think she knew who the love belonged to. The dim blue light illuminated what looked like a box room. She felt a soul connection and turned to see Dave in the corner of the room. He smiled at her and a million sparks of love erupted from her. Dave kneeled down and took a small piece of floorboard out of the floor in the corner beside the wardrobe. She walked over to Dave, who was looking into the hole in the floor. She looked in and saw a gold petty cash box in the floor. Dave put the floorboard back into its place. He smiled again at her and in that smile, she knew that he had passed and she also knew she had a very important message to pass on to his deeply grieving widow, Karen. Dave shook Vicky awake. She woke up and remembered everything; she was so glad as she sometimes forgot the messages. First things first, she needed to tell her ma and her aunty Doris. A plan was needed, she couldn't just go into to a grieving widow's house and blurt out what she had seen in her vision. It was decided by the older women that a period of time needed to pass, since the funeral was only yesterday. A kind of mark of respect for the dead. Also to give Dave's widow time to allow her to grasp the idea that her dead husband had a secret hidden from her! Two weeks was what was decided. Vicky thought it was way too long as she was very curious about what is in that box. Why would he hide it from his lovely wife? Was it too long to help (she had a plan to badger the sisters to make this time shorter). She knew Dave was a loving soul, but she thought that Karen and the family might fall on hard times. What if it was money. They could pay for the funeral. She knew well that having a very helpful soul did not pay the bills or the shopping. His family would miss out on the little bit of money Dave brought in. Sure enough his wife would get the widows pension, but that would mean they could barely scrape by. The funeral bill was probably huge, as burying people was never cheap. Did you ever see an undertaker in a Morris minor? Her ma always said, "When I die, dig a hole in the back garden and put me in and cover me in a few daffs." Vicky was thinking what her ma told her – don't spend money on the dead, money was for the living; it was useless in spirit world. Vicky knew her ma was right.

People go out and buy the nicest coffin (not a phrase you hear every day), plus all the flowers, singers, and all of that stuff that people think shows how much love they had for that person who had passed over. It was about as much use as the smell of the colour grey or the smell from the number seven. She also knew from her connection with spirits that birthdays/anniversaries and the day the person died didn't really have any meaning for the dead, like everybody thought.

Okay the spirit would be stronger at them times, she knew, but they were around all of the time.

People sent energy across the divide by thinking of the dead and that energy was called love. Vicky knew the currency of the universe was love, and it was the same in the spirit world. "Vicky love," her aunty Doris shouted up the stairs. Vicky dropped right back down to Earth. She knew it was time to find out what was in that box.

XI. THE PUB AGAIN

Rachel had only a few hours to go before clocking off for the weekend. She looked forward to the weekends as this is the only thing that was exciting in her shitty life. The last weekend had been a great success, she had nearly came home that weekend with more money than she had gone out with. Also, she had found some money beside the sink in the ladies jax. She could barely remember getting home last week, as she was twisted drunk and eating a kebab with extra sauce! Sarah was her preferred partner in crime, as Rachel knew Sarah's limits and this she used to her advantage.

Vicky was up a few hours by now and had stuffed her face with food. This was very unlike her. She liked to eat but now she was bursting at the seams. A good drop of lotion on the bump was called for to try and save her poor belly from the stretch marks that were already getting worse. A little foot stuck out of the bump as soon as she rubbed it. Was the baby playing with her? The foot was absolutely tiny compared to the size of her hand. Was she ready to become a ma? Vicky was wondering how she got it wrong. This morning when her aunty Doris had called her from downstairs. When she went down the stairs, her ma and Doris had a bag of baby clothes for her. It was added to the pink Babygro's she had bought; they got the baby lovely knitted stuff (pearl cardigans, crochet baby blankets) from the women in Dublin and Manchester (granny clubs). This baby was going to be the bee's knees.

Rachel shaved in the shower, which saved her precious time as Monday morning was moving closer so there wasn't a minute to waste. She had her clothes laid out from the night before, and just had to decide which of two tops to wear. Both of the tops looked really well on her according to the girl in the clothes shop, so she bought the two of them. These were not the type of tops you wore to make yourself feel good. These were man bait tops that showed off enough without not spoiling the surprise. Her plan was to bring a victim home for herself, or, if she could manage it, two!

Vicky was delighted with all the lovely baby clothes. She wondered what she would do with all the pink Babygro's that she bought. She decided to ask the council of elders and she wasn't surprised when the same answer came back twice, so it was decided that the baby would sleep in pink. The kettle had to be put on, after all of that excitement. Two cups of tea and biscuits later, she had a nice surprise for her aunty Doris.

"Aunty Doris," said Vicky.

"Yes love," Doris replied.

"Can I ask you something, a favour really," said Vicky slowly.

This put the watchdogs on high alert. "As long as it's not a lend of money, as I'm smashed," laughed aunty Doris. Doris had a type of *hurry up and just say it* expression, exact same as her sister's face. It was like talking to the same person in two different bodies.

The smell of the perfume investment wafted out of the front door after Rachel, who jumped into the taxi with Sarah already in the back seat. She was trying to put on lipstick and was looking a little rough for want of a better word, but beside Rachel, who was done up to the nines, that was normal. The girls were going to travel a bit further afield for new prey as they had cleared out the local watering holes. A part of town where younger, less experienced prey gathered.

Eventually, the time had come to go to see Dave's widow, Karen. It was decided that Vicky would say nothing and the elders would do the talking. Vicky was going to have to wait to ask her aunty Doris the burning question that she had wanted to ask her earlier as they all got side tracked by a knock on the hall door (it was some lad selling carpets and rugs) and when they got rid of him from the front door, Vicky felt that the moment had passed. Maybe the angels knew of a better time, so it was put off until then. They all crossed the road together heading for a little cake shop. Her ma had said, "I'm not buying flowers, you can't eat flowers." So fresh cream cakes were the order of the day, along with two coffee slices, a custard slice, a chocolate éclair, and a long cream doughnut with raspberry jam in it.

The taxi pulled up and the two girls got a good once over from a group lads out smoking; Sarah barely got a look in because, as they say, she wouldn't get a kick in a stampede. Rachel was a different kettle of fish altogether. The lads liked what was on the menu, not realising that it was them. Sarah didn't give a fuck about what them young lads were thinking, she only wanted a drink or two and a good chin wag with her bestie, probably about work and some boring cunt that worked in that office. Rachel had to listen to the gossip that Sarah told her was happening during the week. It was mind numbingly boring, but Rachel threw in the old sympathy laugh every now and again.

The two elder women went first up the path followed by the Bump, as they had affectionately christened her in the house – slagging your friends was the Dublin way of making them feel better, so she knew it was all a big joke. The door was opened by Romeo, a good looking lad by any standards.

"We're here to see your ma," said me ma as she bashed the useless fucker out of the way.

"She's in the…," he stopped talking since the women were already pouring into the kitchen. He closed the door and flew back up the stairs to continue what he had left off doing.

"Hiya, Karen," said my Ma, "This is me older sister Doris, you know. Remember? She lives in England, she married a lad from Manchester and he died a few years back."

"Ah, Jaysus," says Karen. All the women hugged, and a few tears were shed with snot steaming.

Doris said, "If ya can't show your emotions when someone dies, when can ya?".

Rachel squeezed between two little rides that she had eyed up from the front door, making sure to rub herself all over them like the cheetah does in the Serengeti when it marks its territory. One of the rides near chocked on his peanuts.

"You know they are an aphrodisiac," she said to him.

"I know, that's why I'm eating them," he said.

"Well, if you pay for these drinks, you can put me on the menu for later," she said with a smile. He paid for them drinks and the next few that followed as she was thirsty.

Aunty Doris put on the kettle in Karen's house. She only had the mugs milked and sugared and was just about ready to pour when there was a knock on the door. Romeo must have been up to his usual tricks, because it was at least thirty seconds before they heard him jumping out of the bed and down to the door. It was Sharkey and his missus (people still held him somewhat responsible for Dave's death), no one really knew her name and no one really cared either. They all knew she was a right geebag, so that was the end of that. Vicky wondered why every time she wanted to tell people stuff, she couldn't. Was it perhaps divine timing? She just had to trust and go with it, no use fighting against the Universe.

The night was going exactly as planned. Sarah had gone home about ten minutes ago and Rachel was now stuck in between the two intended targets. The talk turned dirty real fast. So she thought this was the moment to propose to the two lads they both come back to her place. The truth was Rachel lived with her Ma, who was nearly deaf and said "wha" all of the time. she asked the two young lads if they were up for it. One of them chickened out, the better looking lad. She presumed he had a girlfriend, because he was too good looking to be single. "A bird in the hand is worth two in your bush," thought Rachel. Now to get him to pay for the taxi and a chipper on the way back to her den, where she planned to devour him.

The cakes were put onto a big plate by Romeo. "I hope he fuckin washed his hands first," thought the three women as they were sitting in a circle around the cakes. Sharkey's moth made a bee line for the nearest coffee slice. As quick as a flash her ma pulled the whole plate away from her paw.

"Sorry, we didn't know there was going to be people here who didn't bring anything," said me Ma, as her and aunty Doris took their coffee slices. Vicky took the jam doughnut. Karen wasn't eating, which was obvious as she looked like shit, real gaunt-looking, with black bags under both eyes. About five minutes later, after the cakes were gone, the women made their excuses and left. Vicky felt a lot of movement in her belly and down below, maybe the head was engaging. The watchdogs had seen her face and Vicky didn't know what to tell them.

"You okay, Vicky love?" said aunty Doris.

"Yeah it must have been the cake. Too much cream," lied Vicky. She would tell them the truth when they got home, but she would have no need because they knew already.

A local klepto came right up into Rachel's face as she was about to leave the pub. She knew him as he had sold her the perfume she was wearing, it was a near-full bottle of good perfume, with the word TESTER on a label stuck to the bottle, she didn't mind the label, as she paid very little for it until now. She knew she had a good twenty minutes to get rid of him, so she asked him where he'd been.

"I was away on the inside, I stole a chicken and a tin of tomatoes," he said. The judge in the courthouse gave him three months for the chicken and five monts for tomatoes – one month for each tomato in the tin. "I'm just glad I didn't steal a tin of peas." They both had a real good belly laugh. She gave him some loose change, just to be rid of him as she didn't want to be associated with thieves! Her taxi came up and she and her man both jumped in to head back to her place, but first a stop at the takeaway. They shouldn't have bothered; it was as tough as an old Jack Russell.

XII. A NICE SURPRISE

When they got home, Vicky had to run to the toilet
– maybe the baby's head was pressing on her
bladder. She took her time in the toilet so that she
could compose herself before facing the Spanish
inquisition, who she knew was putting on the kettle
right now. Three cups of steaming tea were on the
table when she got downstairs.

"You okay, Vicky love? You turned a funny colour
back there," said the lead inquisitor; her ma was
trying to use x-ray vision to see the baby.

Vicky said the line she had rehearsed in the toilet,
"Yeah, the baby was just moving down below. You

know what I mean?" ssshess (a word pronounced by closing your teeth and breathing in fast through your mouth), like if someone catches a finger in the door!

Her ma's eyeballs went back to normal and she said, "We'll have to go back over tomorrow." They all really wanted to know what was in that box. Vicky had a little bit of doubt. What if she's wrong and they upset Karen for nothing?

"Can I ask ya something? About the baby," said Vicky. Her aunty Doris's head nearly flew off her neck and the x-ray eyes were back. Vicky's next words and tone had to be perfect or else she may get bundled into the back of an ambulance. "Me knickers were wet and there were tiny little spots of blood. So, I changed them and put on a bigger pair."

Aunty Doris was first out of the traps saying, "Sure you should be wearing them skimpy yokes? No soakage in them and you could catch a chill, or worse."

Her ma wasn't going to be outdone. "You should be wearing a big pad, at least at this stage. I don't know if you have started. Have you any pains?"

"Nope, only a little pain in me lower back," said Vicky.

"Mrs Flanagan, next door, went like that on all four of hers. Mine was different; everything just went at once," said my ma.

"Ah, I'd say I'll get away with the big knickers for now," said Vicky. She was thinking them pads are like nappies. Steak and Kidney pies were for dinner, fresh ones straight out of the tin, and not a bleedin' sign of that beautiful corned beef brisket that was mentioned yesterday. She decided to have a warm bath after dinner. She could not stand her usual boiling cauldron bath as it made her feel queasy. The sleep that night was a troubled affair, but before going to sleep she had to rearrange the room for some strange reason. She woke in the morning with more specks of blood on her big knickers.

"How did ya sleep?" asked her ma.

"I was awake at five thirty," said Vicky.

"I was awake a good hour before you," said her ma.

"I was awake at three and I came down for a glass of water and there's the glass I used," said Doris, winning hands down. "Sure you must have heard me, I move around like a bull."

"Bull's right," said her ma. Vicky had to laugh while

pretending to cough. The breakfast was cereal and batch toast. The lunch was crisp sandwiches and chocolate biscuit bars.

"We will pop over to see Karen after lunch and get this mystery over and done with," said me ma, with excitement in her voice. Time went by real slow, as they were all dying to see if it was true. They passed the time reading papers and magazines; Aunty Doris was doing the crossword. "Friction reducers, in four letters and eight letters?" she asked.

Her ma was very helpful and said, "I haven't a clue?"

Baby kicks were getting stronger, but Vicky thought the worst was the head on the bladder and the bum into the lungs.

"Come on and we'll find out what this is," said her ma. So out the door they marched towards Karen's. Vicky presumed it was the same rules as yesterday. Karen answered the door still looking rough and wearing Dave's jumper and socks!

"Come on in, I'll put the kettle on," said Karen.

"Ah don't bother, we just had some," said her ma. "We've come over as we have a bit of a story; a mystery, so to speak.".

Karen looked dazed trying to figure out what was going on. She could remember they were here yesterday, or was that the day before. All the days seemed the same now.

"I'll tell ya what's going on," said her ma; you could hear a pin drop. "Our Vicky had a vision. I'm sorry to say, but it's about Dave. She seen him hiding a small golden box under the floorboards."

Karen was speechless, as expected. Her ma told her where it was, beside the old wooden wardrobe with the mirror. Karen had the response time of a drunk. "That's in my room; what is it, Vicky?" asked Karen. Her ma told her that Vicky didn't know. And that's what they were here to find out.

"I wonder if it's true? And what was Dave up to?"

"Come on, there's only one way to find out," said Karen, jumping up off the chair and flying upstairs. They all followed right on her heels. The room was as Vicky remembered, but the wardrobe was closer to the window. Was it from Dave moving it? There was no carpet on the floor, only a rug which they pushed aside.

"I'll turn on the light," said aunty Doris. Vicky pointed into the corner, they all had a look and saw nothing. Her ma got down on her hands and knees. Nothing, no loose boards, no cuts, nothing. Five minutes standing around, so they went back down to the kitchen, they were discussing what went wrong, if at all? All hope was fading. Vicky sensed a presence, it was Dave.

"You have the right wardrobe, but three months ago it was in the box room," he emoted to her.

Vicky asked, "Could the wardrobe have been moved from the box room?"

Karen's face went white. "It's the wrong fuckin room," said Karen as she flew for the stairs. They were on her like a light, into the box room they all squashed. There was a bag of clothes in the corner, which they moved and straight away they could see a cut in the corner floorboard. they all looked at each other.

"Vicky, you're a good medium, but I suppose you're a large now," said her aunt Doris laughing. Karen bent down and wiggled the board, causing it cave in and inside was a golden box. Karen cried putting her hands to her face. Dave, her Dave, was sending messages to her; she could not hold back the tears. The women waited until Karen composed herself a bit, as they weren't waiting all day. Karen reached in and took out the gold box, which Vicky had seen in her vision. A scream of delight erupted around the room, drawing Romeo from his room. Karen took a deep breath and opened the box. Inside it was Dave's insurance policy, it was taken out two years ago, and an envelope for Karen, The women were all hugging each other. Through the tears of joy and sadness, Karen hugged Vicky for a long time. So glad that they were here, she thanked them from the bottom of her heart while still hugging Vicky. Dave's socks suddenly got drowned by Vicky's baby's waters. In the next fifteen minutes, time went by in a flash, while sitting on the bed, Vicky heard Romeo tell his ma that he knew about the floorboard (the reason Dave hid it was he didn't want people to think he was getting old), but had forgotten as it was so long ago! The ambulance was here and Vicky was hooked up to the gas. The three women flew down to Holles Street in the ambulance.

The fire was down to the red embers and the sitting room was nice and warm enough not to have a stitch of clothes on. Both of them were as naked as the day they were born. Rachel's ma was in bed, with no fear of her coming down as she was cocooned and never moved until morning. She was also a little hard of hearing but wasn't deaf, so the telly was put on low. A nature program, something about praying mantis. She hated creepy crawlies. The female praying mantis ate the male's head during mating. "Interesting," she thought as she looked at her prey. He was well drunk, lying down on her sofa with his feet sticking over the arm. She kneeled on the floor in front of the sofa, halfway down his body (on the nice, thick rug she had moved there earlier that day). She had already explained the rules to him in the taxi. She bent over, the embers from the fire warmed her and she liked it. He was already moaning, she stopped to remind him again, and as he grabbed her by the hair, he agreed, so she continued. She could hear the female mantis devouring the torso. "Snap," she thought. She continued in the hope that the male could control himself, as she was very good at this. If he couldn't here, then he wouldn't be suitable for there. She could hear that the poor male was half eaten and this was when he passed his sperm over, when he was dead. Rachel never noticed her prey's toes curling upwards. She felt a pulse too late. "Ya dirty bastard," she said, trying to get out of the way as he pulsed all over her ma's sitting room. It landed in her hair, on her back, on the top of the sofa (and on the clock on the mantle, which wouldn't be found for weeks). She would be cleaning forever, she thought. She gathered up his clothes and fucked him out, naked, shutting the hall door. She cleaned in her good knickers and bra. The praying mantis was also cleaning its claws after its first meal which would sustain their young.

Sharkey climbed out of the bed. He was very tired, even though it was already ten-thirty and he was usually up at seven. He had not sleep since the tragic accident. "Why did Dave not learn to swim," he thought. He was sad that one of his friends was dead; it didn't matter how, he just was. Sharkey's moth was a lazy bitch, too lazy to scratch herself. She had nine hours of good snoring, and he knew because he timed the hippo. She was still there when he got out. He put the kettle on and leaned on the sink. Looking out of the window, he noticed his reflection and he didn't care that his jock needed changing. The tea was made and he put extra sugar in and just a drop of milk. He was thinking 'what if scenarios' for the hundredth time that day. His mind was not his own. He could not control his thoughts. He felt guilty for Dave's death and, on top of that, he had decided to let his other friend drown. What kind of a person was he turning into; was he changing into that yoke upstairs? He had made decisions with very little time and had to live with the consequences for a very long time. This was not fair, what do people think when they looked at him? Fuck them, those pricks would do the same in his shoes, wouldn't they? Jabba the Hut was awake.

"Is there tea for me? And bring up six slices of toast with loads of butter," said the sloth. He threw the toast on, topped up his tea from the pot, and brought her up six slices of ghost (that's what she called barely done toast). He didn't give a fuck, he was out of there. The swill he brought would not last long, so he moved real fast, not even changing his jocks. He had to get out, the shops for the paper was the ticket and he might not come back. Sharkey walked into the newsagents and picked up a cheap rag tabloid (it was named after the biggest body in the solar system, no not the hippo).

"Howaya." It was Eddy form the bar "I'd say your fuckin' relieved, to hear the news."
"About what?" asked Sharkey.

"It seems Dave had a heart attack and didn't drown after all," said Eddy, giving Sharkey his old life back. Eddy smiled at him, as he noticed the reaction on Sharkey's face, patting him on the shoulder and shouting to the girl behind the counter, "Ham salad roll, love." Eddy was a charmer, a big hit with the ladies. He always got extra ham. Sharkey stood by the papers, crying; he was off the hook, it wasn't his fault.

The ambulance brought the three of them to the hospital. There were really four as Aunty June was there and this had a calming effect on her. Vicky's pains were very mild. She was brought into an examination room and they weren't waiting long before the doctor arrived. All the women left, even June, and ten minutes later the nurse called the three of them back in. Only two through the door, though. The nurse said it wouldn't be long. The women were ready to explode with excitement. The women got to work, keeping Vicky occupied and the time passed nicely with the nurse in every half hour.

Vicky was now in pain. She held onto that gas for dear life; gone out the door was the essential oils, her ma and Doris disappeared at least once an hour. "They must have bladder problems," she thought. Aunty June never moved, she just kept smiling. Her ma and Doris were great, bringing back cups of tea and rubbing her back, which seemed to hurt the most. Around eight her waters fully went and a midwife came in.

"Let's have a look; very good," she said. The pains came real strong after that, and the urge to push soon after. The midwife said, "I can see baby's hair." Doris was crying and squeezed Vicky's hand as she looked in her eyes with a smile. The contractions were building and in between one Vicky said to Doris, "I would be delighted if, (contraction, now it's over), you would be the baby's godmother." She stuck her chin down and pushed.

"And again," said the midwife. Vicky felt a stinging pain down below. "One big push now, well done. Baby is born, you have a little boy." said the midwife.

Vicky look up to see her ma and Doris holding onto each other, crying their eyes out. The next few hours passed by in a strange feeling kind of way. The baby was beside her in the bed, swaddled in a blue blanket with a pink Babygro on.

"Any idea of a name, now that you have seen him?" asked her ma.

"Yeah, I'm calling him Dean," she said. The tears flood between the women, washing away a lot of pain and suffering. That night was one which they will not forget for a very long time. Aunty June smiled at Dean and he smiled back.

NOTE 1

The letter from Dave, which was in the box.

Karen,

Should you be reading this note, it means I am dead. Know this – I will love you until the end of time. I know you have loved me as no one else has done.

The insurance policy was always something I had meant to get, but just kept putting it off. I hope there is enough to keep you in the luxury that you are used to; there should be enough to send Luke (Romeo) to college.

Love always,

Dave

NOTE 2

Siobhan heard about the ambulance. She came to the hospital to visit her friend and the new baby, but she was stopped in the corridor. She would have had a better chance of getting past The Berlin Wall. Her ma and aunty Doris tore her to shreds for a full fifteen minutes while Siobhan stood with her mouth closed. Vicky didn't think she would be seeing her again, ha.

ABOUT THE AUTHOR

Hello, I am Harold Wynne, I live with my wife, Karen and children, Craig, Luke, Jade, Becki and Shannon in County Wexford, Ireland.

Born into a family of ten children, with Psychic abilities (of which all have shunned them, except me).

Medium Psychic and Tarot Card reader, Bio Energy Healer, Reiki Master, Black Belt in Hapkido (and Karaoke), Planetary Science from Open University, CBT Practitioner from Udemy, Boat Fisherman, Gardener, and general dreamer.

This is my first book; I wrote it to try and materialise my feelings about grief and loosing loved ones. I really hope this book comes across saying, that even in our darkest times, they are with us, they love us and they always will, they mind us until we get to meet up with them again, one day.
I hope you like it Har and Da…

CONTACT THE AUTHOR

If you do wish to contact me about the book, please do write to my email address:

Haroldwynne70@gmail.com